Ella Hu   drawing.

She graduate   in illustration
and   erself.

                                                     1.

For my mum,
and with a special thank you to all my tutors
at University College Falmouth – E.H.

Hudson HATES School

ELLA HUDSON

F
FRANCES LINCOLN
CHILDREN'S BOOKS

Hudson loved making things.
He liked painting pictures and building models
and baking cakes. He liked sewing too!

But there was one thing
that Hudson really hated . . .

It was Friday morning and Hudson remembered why he had especially NOT wanted to go to school that day. . .

"Spelling TEST today, Hudson."

Hudson had not learnt his spellings.

Miss French read out the words and Hudson felt his heart sink. The other children at his desk started to snigger.

Next they had to swap books and mark each other's spellings. This was what Hudson had been dreading most of all.

The bell sounded. It was break time!
"Well done, everyone," said Miss French.

"Now, when I read out your name,
shout out your score and
you can go outside and play."

Ha ha!

Ha!!
Ha!!

It came to Hudson's turn and everyone started to giggle.

For yet another Friday break time
Hudson was sitting inside writing out his spellings.

When he saw his mum at the gate,
Hudson just couldn't hold in his tears
any longer.

I...am never going back to school... ever again!

On the way home
Hudson told his mum
about his horrible day,
and how he dreaded school.

When they got home,
the phone rang.
It was Miss French.

The following Monday at school, a man
came into the classroom with Miss French.
He had a briefcase and was wearing a lizard tie.

Hudson, this is Mr Shapland.
He is going to take you into
the study room and give
you a quick test.

Hudson had had enough.

When Hudson had calmed down,
he and Mr Shapland went to the study room.

"This is a different kind of test, Hudson,"
explained Mr Shapland. "You won't be
in trouble because there are no right
or wrong answers."

Mr Shapland showed Hudson a series of pictures and asked him what he thought was missing from each of them. He had some funny-shaped triangle blocks, and he asked Hudson to make patterns with them.

Mr Shapland also recorded Hudson's results on a machine.

This isn't so bad!

The test wasn't bad at all – in fact
it was better than any Hudson had ever had!

Mr Shapland explained to Hudson why he found it
hard to learn as quickly as his classmates.
It was because he had a learning difficulty
called dyslexia.

Dyslexia affects people differently. Often they tend to be more creative than others.

Mr Shapland's brain

People that do **not** have **dyslexia** use the **left** side of their brain for sorting out **words** and **numbers**. They use the **right** side of their brain for creative tasks, like **drawing** and making things. They may find learning easier than people with dyslexia, because their brain tends to use each side **equally**.

Hudson's brain

People **with dyslexia** don't balance the work between both sides of the brain. They use the **right** side of their brain for sorting out **words** and **numbers**. They may find all of those things difficult, because their brains have to work up to **six** times harder than someone without dyslexia.

A week later, the school arranged for Hudson to have some of his lessons in a different classroom. The other children there also had dyslexia.

For these lessons they had a new teacher,
who had lots of fun and exciting ways
to help them to learn.

Soon Hudson's schoolwork really improved.
At last school wasn't something that Hudson hated.
He actually began to quite like it!

Dyslexia is a learning difficulty that mainly affects reading and spelling. People with dyslexia tend to have difficulties in dealing with word-sounds and problems with short-term verbal memory, sequencing and organisation. Its effects may be seen in spoken and written language. Studies suggest that, in dyslexic people, the connections between different language areas of the brain do not work as well as they should.

These differences are not linked to intelligence, and many dyslexic people have strengths and abilities in tasks that involve creative and visual thinking.

Dyslexic people usually find it difficult to work with the sounds of spoken words, and many have difficulties with short-term memory. This means that it is more difficult for them to spell and 'sound out' words.

Dyslexia is not the same as a problem with reading. Many dyslexic people learn to read, but have continuing difficulties with spelling, writing, memory and organisation. There are also people whose difficulties with reading are not caused by dyslexia. Dyslexia can also cause problems in maths.

Dyslexia should not be a barrier to achievement and success if it is properly recognised, and steps are taken to provide suitable teaching and training.

Resources
The British Dyslexic Association - www.bdadyslexia.org.uk
Dyslexia Action - www.dyslexiaaction.org.uk
Dyslexia USA - www.dyslexia-usa.com
Dyslexia Australia and New Zealand - http://www.dyslexia-parent.com/australia.html

Hudson Hates School copyright © Frances Lincoln Limited 2010
Text and illustrations copyright © Ella Hudson 2010
The right of Ella Hudson to be identified as the author and illustrator
of this work has been asserted by her in accordance with the Copyright,
Designs and Patents Act, 1988 (United Kingdom).

First published in Great Britain in 2010 and the USA in 2011 by
Frances Lincoln Children's Books, 4 Torriano Mews,
Torriano Avenue, London NW5 2RZ
www.franceslincoln.com

First paperback edition published in Great Britain in 2012.

A catalogue record for this book is available from the British Library.

ISBN 978-1-84780-375-7

Illustrated with ink, watercolour and pencil.

Set in Fiendstar.
**This typeface was designed to increase legibility, making it especially suitable
for people who have difficulties with reading.**

Printed in China.

1 2 3 4 5 6 7 8 9

MORE TITLES FROM FRANCES LINCOLN CHILDREN'S BOOKS

ONCE UPON A TIME
Niki Daly

Sarie doesn't like school. Every time she has to take out her reading book, her voice disappears and the other children tease her. But one person understands how she feels – Ou Missus, an old lady living across the veld, who tells wonderful stories. . .

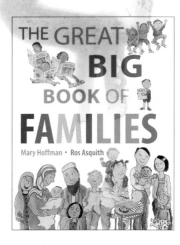

LOOKING AFTER LOUIS
Lesley Ely
Illustrated by Polly Dunbar

"There's a new boy at school called Louis. He's not quite like the rest of us. If I ask him what he's looking at he just says, 'Looking at' and carries on looking." This introduction to the issue of autism shows how – through imagination, kindness, and a special game of football – Louis's classmates find a way to join him in his world. Then they can include Louis in theirs.

THE GREAT BIG BOOK OF FAMILIES
Mary Hoffman
Illustrated by Ros Asquith

Families come in all shapes and sizes – and this book takes a look at all the different kinds, featuring homes and holidays, schools and pets, feelings and family trees – and lots more. . .

Frances Lincoln titles are available from all good bookshops.
You can also buy books and find out more about your favourite titles,
authors and illustrators on our website: www.franceslincoln.com